More books about Kipper

In **January**
Kipper took a picture with
his new camera and made
a New Year Resolution,
'This year I will not throw
any snowballs at Tiger.'
And for a whole month
he kept his
promise…

Because the snow did not fall until

February!

An icicle grew on Kipper's house. It lasted for three weeks and grew to 87 centimetres.

Kipper took a photograph.

In **March** the wind flapped Kipper's ears.

It straightened his scarf and scruffled the daffodils on Big Hill. Then it blew Tiger right off his feet!

Click!
This is the picture that Kipper took.

Soon the
pond in the
park was full
of croaking and wriggling
and glooping and jiggling.
'March is the froggiest
month,' said Kipper.

'But April is best
for catching tadpoles.'

In June Kipper lay on his back and watched as little things with legs and wings climbed the spindly grasses and whizzed into the big, blue sky.

'There are a lot more little things with legs and wings than you would think,' thought Kipper.

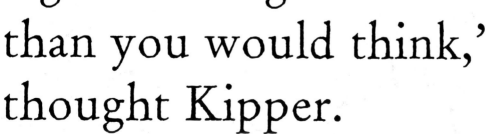

The first week in
July was hot.
The second week
was hotter still.

And then **Boom!**

Booom!

Booom!

A thunderstorm!

August was

summer holiday time.

Kipper took a parachute
ride above the sea.
'Take my
picture!'
he called
to Tiger.

In September the bramble bushes were full of blackberries.

The thorns were prickly. 'Ouch! Ouch!' But the blackberries were delicious.

'Mmmmmmmmm!'

In **October**
Kipper and Tiger made a
collection of autumn things.

'October is an orangey
brown sort of month,'
said Tiger.

They made a face from
the pumpkin
which
glowed in
the dark.

November

came around, and twiggy branches made patterns against the misty moon.

They huffed their breath into the heavy garden air, seeing who could huff the highest.

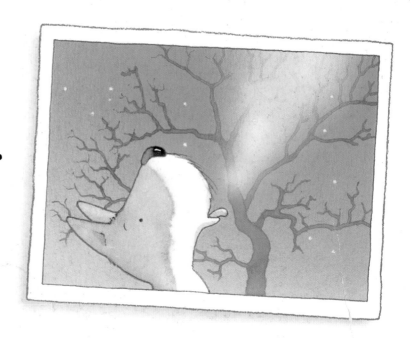

In **December**
the days grew dark and cold.

Kipper stayed indoors making decorations and a special Christmas present for Tiger.

'I need one more photograph,' said Kipper.

So he called Tiger and got out his camera.

'Smile!'

said Kipper as
he opened the
front door.

But Tiger was
already smiling,
because it was snowing,
and because he had not
forgotten about February.

Click! went Kipper's
camera.

Booof!
went Tiger's snowball!

What we did this y

...ary

February

march

May

June

July

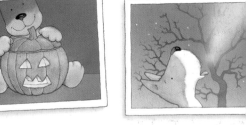

September

October

Novembe...